THIS BOOK BELONGS TO:

SECRET IDENTITY

Do not fill this bit in or
Dr Septic will know who you are
....

SUPERHERO NAME

....

JOHNNY CATBISCUIT

TO THE RESCUE!

MICHAEL COX

ILLUSTRATED BY GARY DUNN

EGMONT

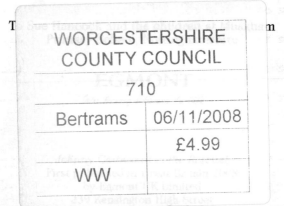

London W8 6SA

Text copyright © Michael Cox 2008
Illustrations copyright © Gary Dunn 2008

The moral rights of the author and illustrator have been asserted

ISBN 978 1 4052 3736 9

1 3 5 7 9 10 8 6 4 2

A CIP catalogue record for this title is available from the British Library

Printed and bound in Great Britain by the CPI Group

CONTENTS

CHAPTER ONE - HIDE AND SQUEAK 1

CHAPTER TWO - ANIMAL PROTECTION MAN 9

CHAPTER THREE - THE THUGS 20

CHAPTER FOUR - A REAL HALFWIT! 34

CHAPTER FIVE - DEAR DINGBAT 39

CHAPTER SIX - JOHNNY CATBISCUIT! 50

CHAPTER SEVEN - SUPERHERO SUPPORT SERVICE SOLUTION ...57

CHAPTER EIGHT - DR SEPTIC 65

CHAPTER NINE - TIME FOR ACTION! 78

CHAPTER TEN - SQUEAK! SQUEAK! 90

CHAPTER ELEVEN - TONGUES 97

CHAPTER TWELVE - FELIX PAWSON 108

CHAPTER THIRTEEN - WHOOOOOOOOOOSH! 120

SUPERHERO PROFILE - ANIMAL PROTECTION MAN 132

VILLAIN PROFILE - DR SEPTIC 138

EXTRACT FROM KERPOW! - THE ULTIMATE SUPERHERO'S HANDBOOK

UNCOVER YOUR INNER SUPERHERO...144

CHAPTER ONE
HIDE AND SQUEAK

When twelve-year-old Wayne Bunn got out of bed on that sunny Sunday morning, he had no idea that it would turn out to be the most mind-boggling day of his life! A day in which he would see and do things which he would never before have believed possible. After all, Wayne was only a very ordinary boy, with a very ordinary life, and very ordinary abilities. But all that . . . was about to change!

Wayne lived with his gran in Nicetown, in the rather picturesque and pleasant country known as the Realms of Normality. During his school holidays, he helped out at her little pet shop on Nicetown High Street. On Saturdays he worked at the Nicetown Animal Rescue Shelter. And he spent his Sundays playing with his kitten, Miss Purrfect, and his baby rabbit, Warren. When he wasn't busy doing those things, he'd be taking his beloved spaniel, Mr Parks, for long walks, hoping to find distressed and lost wild creatures, so that he could comfort them, or simply offer them directions.

Yes, Wayne was absolutely nuts about animals.

And that was what was going to change his life
. . . forever!

On the Sunday morning in question, Wayne
and Mr Parks were in the park, playing hide-
and-squeak. First, Mr Parks would rush off with
a squeaky rubber bone and hide. Then Wayne
would go and look for Mr Parks, who would stay
as quiet as he could (which isn't easy with a
squeaky rubber bone in your mouth). Then it
would be Wayne's turn to hide.

They'd been playing for ten minutes and
Wayne was looking for a hiding place, when a
bush said, 'Psssst! You with the squeaky bone!'

Wayne let out a big squeak, dropped the bone

and stood there, open-mouthed in amazement.
Then he rubbed his eyes and saw that the
bush wasn't a bush, but a small, bearded man

wearing a camouflage outfit.

The man smiled and said, 'Wayne Bunn?'

'Yes, I am,' said Wayne. 'But who are you?'

The man looked around nervously, then whispered, 'I'd rather not say right now. But I've heard all about you. For instance, I know that you are an orphan who lives with his gran. And that she is in hospital with a poorly heart. But, Wayne, the main thing that's been brought to my attention is your extraordinary kindness to animals. Do you remember that daddy-long-legs you found with the broken leg?'

'Oh!' said Wayne. 'Graham!'

'Is that what you called him?' said the man.

'Well, what really struck me was the way you nursed Graham back to health. And even taught him to walk again!'

'Then accidentally sat on him and squashed him,' said Wayne.

'Then accidentally sat on him and squashed him,' agreed the man. 'But we all make mistakes, Wayne. However, what has most impressed me is your amazing courage! Do you remember how you leapt into the lake to save that drowning parrot?'

'Which turned out to be a duck,' said Wayne.

'Well, yes,' said the man. 'But that's not the point, Wayne. You heroically plunged into

deep, icy water with no thought for your own
safety. And you can't even swim!'

'I couldn't just stand by and watch a poor
creature drown,' said Wayne.

'Well, Wayne Bunn!' said the man. 'I have
great news for you. You are to have a new role
in life! One that will test your skill and courage
to the limit.'

Then he opened his jacket to reveal three
tiny labrador puppies staring up at him from
one of the big inside pockets, while a lamb, two
ducklings and a one-eyed tortoise gazed up at
him from the other, their eyes aglow with love
and trust.

'**SHUDDERING SPIDER-CRABS!**' gasped Wayne. 'You're . . . you're . . . Animal Protection Man!'

CHAPTER TWO
ANIMAL PROTECTION MAN

'Yes, Wayne, I am Animal Protection Man. And no doubt you have heard of my many daring exploits and heroic deeds.'

'Oh yes, I have, Animal Protection Man!' cried Wayne. 'Not to mention the daring deeds of all the other superheroes who guard the Realms of Normality: **DANGER DUDE**, Susan the Human-Post-It-Note, *Hillman Avenger*, Time-Slip Sandra, **Captain Unstoppable**, and lots, lots more!'

Then, gazing at Animal Protection Man with a look of undisguised awe and admiration, he said, 'But, Animal Protection Man, out of all of the superheroes, you are my number one! My absolute favourite! You couldn't be anything else! Not when I think of all the thousands of innocent creatures you've rescued from the wicked humans who make their lives a misery!'

'It's very nice of you to say so, Wayne!' replied Animal Protection Man with a modest shrug. But then he looked grave and said, 'However, I am old now. And my superpowers are on the wane, Wayne.'

'On the Wayne Wayne?' said Wayne.

'Yes, Wayne, the wane, Wayne,' said Animal Protection Man. 'They are fading fast and will soon be gone forever.'

'Oh, that's terrible!' said Wayne.

'Yes, I know. And not just for me. Only a couple of hours ago, my pooped-out powers forced me to abandon the most important rescue operation I have ever undertaken!'

'Oh no!' gasped Wayne. 'What was it?'

'An attempt to free hundreds of stolen pets from the secret experimental laboratories of Dr Septic!' said Animal Protection Man.

At the mention of that name, Wayne went cold all over. On the whole of Space-Speck

Earth, no person was more feared, loathed or despised than the evil genius Dr Septacemius J. Septic. In every city, town and village of the Realms of Normality, Dr Septic and his malicious mob of malevolent mates, satanic subordinates and creepy cronies were known as all that was loathsome and foul. For as long as people could remember, he and his abominable associates – Murgatroyd Doom, Sticky Billy, Elvis Troll and Janice Evil, to name but a few – had been causing all manner of turmoil and distress. And it was only due to the courage, selflessness and constant vigilance of the superheroes that Dr Septic had never yet

managed to fulfil his evil desire: to take over the Realms and enslave all the good and decent and honest and hardworking people and animals who lived there.

Even when Wayne was little, his gran used to say to him, 'If you're bad, Dr Septic will get you!' But Wayne never was bad. It was Dr Septic who was constantly wicked. And nothing had changed.

'Yes,' continued Animal Protection Man, 'the vile Dr Septic has embarked on yet another of his perfidious plans to wreak havoc and misery amongst our furry friends. This time aided by his wicked accomplice, the evil puppy-rancher

13

St Bernard Muttshoes!'

'Is he the one who makes the really comfy footwear?' said Wayne.

The three tiny labradors suddenly began to whimper with terror.

'Hush, puppies!' said Animal Protection Man. 'Yes, Wayne, he is the same St Bernard Muttshoes. He and Dr Septic are attempting to create all sorts of unnatural monstrosities in those nightmarish laboratories of theirs. I will not go into detail, but if I say self-plucking chickens and yodelling mice, I think you'll get the idea!'

'Uurgh, gross!' gasped Wayne. 'But how did

you find out?'

'Let's just say a little bird told me,' said Animal Protection Man, with a knowing wink.

'Oh, I get you!' said Wayne. 'You don't want to tell me, do you?'

'No!' said Animal Protection Man. 'A little bird really did tell me! I talk with the animals. And that is how I got the information for my daring rescue plan. However, at a most crucial moment my superpowers failed me. So I was only able to save these little chaps.'

The animals all yapped and bleated and quacked in thanks; apart from the one-eyed tortoise, which remained very quiet

and thoughtful.

'But,' continued Animal Protection Man, 'what I saw in those loathsome labs has given me enough evidence to put St Bernard and Dr Septic away forever. And, most importantly of all, as I fled, I managed to snatch . . . this!'

He reached into his pocket and took out a tiny plastic bottle. Inside it was some strange pinkish-green slime which glowed and bubbled eerily.

'This, Wayne,' announced Animal Protection Man, 'is the world's entire stock of the rare, double-stranded DNA chromosome, commonly known as **GUNGE**[*]! Put to good use, **GUNGE** can cure the worst of illnesses. For

[*] GOBSMACKINGINGLY USEFUL NOVELTY GENE ENZYME

16

17

instance, your gran's poorly heart. However, in the wrong hands anything is possible.'

'Oh no!' gasped Wayne.

'Yes, anything! But I have the **GUNGE**! And without it those evil fiends cannot complete their diabolical experiments.'

Animal Protection Man twitched a couple of times and wiped a bead of sweat from his forehead. Then, glancing anxiously around him, he whispered, 'But, Wayne, even as we speak, their thugs are hot on my trail. It will only be a matter of minutes before they catch up with me! And sadly, I no longer have the strength to resist them!'

'Oh no!' muttered Wayne, looking more worried by the second.

'So, Wayne,' continued Animal Protection Man, 'the moment has come for me to hand over my duties. To someone young, courageous and kind. Someone who will risk everything to continue the fight against St Bernard Muttshoes, the evil Dr Septic and their like. And Wayne, you . . . are that someone!'

CHAPTER THREE
THE THUGS!

'Wayne Bunn!' said Animal Protection Man. 'From this day on, you will be known as . . . *JOHNNY CATBISCUIT!*'

'*OO-ER!*' gasped Wayne.

Animal Protection Man now produced a black bin liner, saying, 'Wayne, this may look like an ordinary bin liner. But it contains your future! Yes, Wayne, your very own superhero outfit, made to fit you perfectly. Now!' he

continued, looking very anxious . . .'time is pressing! Those fiends will be here at any moment! Listen carefully, Wayne! Once you put on this super-suit and say the words:

Be kind to your moggies and pamper your doggies
And Johnny will leave you be
But if you duff up your pups, or tease your bees
You'll answer to Johnny C!'

you will instantly possess awesome superpowers. For example, you will be able to swim underwater for hours on end, cutting the nets of fishing boats, freeing millions of trapped kippers and unhooking prize-winning sticklebacks from the cruel barbs of sports anglers. All without your

skin going pruney!'

'Wow!' exclaimed Wayne.

'And!' continued Animal Protection Man. 'Just like me, you will be able to zoom through the skies, flying to the rescue!'

'Cor!' gasped Wayne.

'And finally, Wayne,' said Animal Protection Man, producing a tiny silver widget, 'this little beauty is a biometric, plasma-chuffed wrist-pod. Simply use it to contact **SSSS** whenever you have a problem or a question.'

'**SSSS?**' said Wayne.

'Superhero Support Service Solutions!' said Animal Protection Man. 'Just dial *W-0000-SH* and

press the hash key. Then choose *OPTION 6*!'

'Cool!' said Wayne, as Animal Protection Man slipped the wrist-pod into the bin liner.

'But, Wayne,' continued Animal Protection Man. 'You must not breathe a word to anyone about what you have seen or heard here today. St Bernard and Dr Septic have spies everywhere. Even in the Police Force, the British Vole Society and the Kennel Club. So, not a word, Wayne!'

'No, not a word!' repeated Wayne. 'I promise!'

'So, Wayne, what do you say?' said Animal Protection Man. 'Will you continue my caped crusade to save our animal friends?'

Wayne scratched his head for a moment. Then he frowned, took a deep breath and said, 'Er, no thanks. I'd rather not!'

'What!' cried Animal Protection Man.

'I'd rather not,' said Wayne. 'It's very nice of you to offer. But I don't think I'm the sort of person you're looking for.'

'But why ever not?'

Wayne blushed, then said, 'To be honest with you, a lot of people think I'm a bit of a twit. I'm most definitely not up to the job of being Johnny Gingerbiscuit!'

'Catbiscuit,' said Animal Protection Man.

'Yes, him!' said Wayne. 'I'm really sorry to

disappoint you, Animal Protection Man. I'm sure you'll find someone else. I'll be off now. It's time for Mr Parks' din-dins!'

He put the lead on Mr Parks and began to walk away.

'But, Wayne!' cried Animal Protection Man, rushing after him and thrusting the bin liner into his arms. 'Think of the excitement! The adventures!'

'No, I can't do it, Animal Protection Man!' protested Wayne. 'I'm a complete birdbrain! I'd make a pig's dinner of the whole thing. There are bound to be much better Johnny Dogbiscuits around than I could ever be!'

'But, Wayne!' pleaded Animal Protection Man. 'The creatures of the world need –'

He never finished his sentence.

At that moment there was a huge roar and a massive **iSPLATZ-U**™ 4x4 vehicle screeched to a halt in the trees about thirty metres away. It was carrying a large cage and . . . horror of horrors, strapped to its massive front bumper bars, was a very unhappy-looking sausage dog!

Three enormous, extremely thuggish-looking men climbed out of the **iSPLATZ-U**™. They were wearing fur hats, moleskin trousers and leather coats and were casually chewing roasted chicken legs.

Mr Parks began to growl bravely, while all the little creatures in Animal Protection Man's pockets squeaked and cried with terror. Apart from the one-eyed tortoise, which just remained very quiet and thoughtful.

'Crikey!' whispered Wayne. 'What an evil-looking bunch!'

'More evil than you can imagine!' said Animal Protection Man. Then, grasping Wayne by the shoulder, he said, 'Wayne! I am so, so, so sorry that you were unable to accept the challenge of becoming Johnny Catbiscuit. It will be:

A terrible loss to all creatures great and small.
Both the horse in its stable and the cow in its stall,
The hen in its hen house and the furry field mouse,
The burrowing wombat and the humble woodlouse,
The squawking cockatoo and the wolf in its lair,
The bouncy kangaroo and the great grizzly bear.'

Wayne suddenly got the feeling that this 'lament' might go on for some time.

But then Animal Protection Man glanced over his shoulder and saw that the thuggish-looking men were running towards them. His theme changed!

'*Now Dr Septic wants his potion.*
So I'd better be in motion.
I'm sorry, young Bunn, but I really must run.
And then I will fly. Farewell, good Wayne!
Bye bye!'

As he recited these lines, Animal Protection Man underwent the most astonishing metamorphosis. First his body changed. In just seconds he went from being a rather normal little man to a squat and muscular, barrel-chested hunk. He might

well have been an Olympic international weightlifter, or shot-putter. Then he literally '**EXPLODED**' out of his drab and tatty camouflage outfit, revealing a magnificent midnight blue leather flying suit, emblazoned with the beautiful golden logo **APM**.

With Wayne and Mr Parks watching in open-mouthed amazement, he galloped off across the park, flapping his arms wildly. The brutish-looking thugs gave chase, and Wayne dodged behind a bush. He watched the pursuit from there, protectively hugging his beloved Mr

31

Parks to his chest.

The thugs were soon gaining on Animal Protection Man. But then, just when it looked like they would surely catch him, his strides suddenly began to get **BIGGER . . . AND BIGGER . . . AND BIGGER!** An instant later, he leapt into the air and stretched out his arms in front of him. As he did, there was a sudden **WHOOOOSH!** noise, and trails of blue smoke began to pour from the ends of his trouser legs. Three seconds after that, he angled his body at forty-five degrees to the earth, banked slightly and shot towards the treetops, like a rocket zooming off to the stratosphere,

leaving the thugs fuming with frustration.

'Phew!' sighed Wayne, as he watched his hero soar skywards. 'Thank goodness for that! Way to go, Animal Protection Man!'

But Wayne's relief was short-lived.

CHAPTER FOUR
a Real Halfwit!

As Animal Protection Man was passing over the trees where the thugs had parked their **iSPLATZ-U**™, he gave a cry of pain, clutched his shoulder and groaned, 'Oooh, my bad back!'

Then, to Wayne's total dismay, he suddenly stopped soaring and crashed into the trees. He ended up dangling about three metres above the ground, upside-down! He desperately struggled to free himself, while the thugs raced

up to him, laughing cruelly. There was a great **YAPPING** and QUACKING and **BLEATING** and Wayne watched in horror as the poor rescued pets tumbled from Animal Protection Man's pockets straight into the arms of the thugs, who roughly hurled them into the cage on the **iSPLATZ-U**™.

The thugs now began violently shaking the tree in which Animal Protection Man was entangled. After a few moments he plunged to the ground and the biggest of the thugs picked him up by his ears, while another began searching him and yelling, 'Where's the **GUNGE**, fungus-face? What have you done with it?'

35

'Do your worst!' groaned Animal Protection Man. 'I'll never tell you!

With that, the sleazeballs began giving him Chinese burns and tweaking his nose really viciously. Wayne could hardly bear to watch.

'He must have hidden it just after he escaped from the secret laboratory,' said the smallest

thug. 'It could be anywhere!'

'No worries!' laughed the big thug. 'I've got just the thing to jog his memory!'

Mr Parks trembled in Wayne's arms as the thug produced a huge and fearsome-looking syringe, saying, 'Once he's had a blast of this, we'll soon have the truth out of him. Dr Septic's special serum never fails. Put him in the car. You drive, and I'll get *stuck* in!'

'What are we going to do about that dumb-looking kid?' said the third thug. 'The one we saw him talking to when we arrived.'

'Ha!' laughed the big thug. 'There's no way he'll be a problem. He was obviously a

complete dingbat!'

'Yeah, a real halfwit!' echoed his brutish pal. 'A total loser if ever I saw one!'

Wayne winced, then stared at his feet and blushed from head to toe.

Sensing his master's discomfort, Mr Parks began to lick Wayne's face affectionately.

'OK . . . let's hit the road!' said the big thug.

'I'd sooner hit some kittens!' laughed his pal.

'Me too!' agreed the third one. 'But there'll be plenty of time for that later!'

CHAPTER FIVE
DEAR DINGBAT . . .

'Oh no!' thought Wayne, as he watched the **iSPLATZ-U**™ roar away. 'What am I going to do now?'

His first impulse was to dash to the police station and report everything he'd seen. Then he remembered that Animal Protection Man had said no one could be trusted. And he suddenly felt very frightened and very lonely.

So, what was he to do? He supposed he could tell his gran. But the shock might be too

much for her. As he agonised, he felt a tug on the lead and looked down to see Mr Parks staring up at him with his tongue hanging out. Wayne looked at his watch.

'Flying flip-flops!' he exclaimed. 'It's way past dinnertime. I bet you're starving, Mr Parks. Miss Purrfect and Warren will be too!'

Well, that was that! Wayne's pets came first. He'd never let *them* down! So, his first job was to dash home and feed them. And to pop into the supermarket for some catfood on the way. And while he was doing that he would decide who to tell about Animal Protection Man.

When he got to the supermarket, Wayne tied Mr Parks' lead to the railing by the trolleys, saying, 'I'll be two ticks!' Then he joked, 'Don't go away!'

Wayne could only have been in the supermarket

41

for about three minutes, but, as he came out, he immediately knew that something was wrong. Something about Mr Parks seemed different. He looked longer. And thinner. And he wasn't moving! It was then that Wayne realised he wasn't actually looking at Mr Parks. Because Mr Parks was gone! And in his place was the sausage dog which Wayne had last seen strapped to the bumper of the **iSPLATZ-U**™! The sausage dog which Wayne could now see wasn't a real sausage dog at all, but one of those stuffed sausage-dog-shaped draught excluders that his gran liked. Then Wayne spotted the note which was pinned to the sausage dog's ear.

And his eyes filled with tears.

DEAR DINGBAT
YOU SHOULD HAVE CALLED YOUR DOG STEWART.
OR 'STEW' FOR SHORT. AS IN 'DOG STEW'! WHICH
IS WHAT WE'LL MAKE HIM INTO IF YOU DON'T
GIVE US THE 'YOU-KNOW-WHAT'! YES, WE
KNOW YOU'VE GOT IT! ANIMAL PROTECTION
MAN TOLD US JUST BEFORE HE . . . 'WENT'!
WE ALSO KNOW YOU'VE GOT A LOVELY
KITTEN AND A LIKKLE BUNNY WABBIT! AND WE
KNOW WHERE YOU LIVE. HA! HA! SEE YOU SOON!

Wayne's brain whirled with fear and confusion. The thugs must be mistaken. He hadn't got the 'YOU-KNOW-WHAT'.

Or had he? All at once Wayne remembered feeling something unfamiliar in his pocket when he'd reached for his money in the supermarket. Something small and plastic! He thrust his hand into his pocket and pulled it out. In his palm lay the tiny bottle of **GUNGE**!

Wayne's mouth went dry and his pulse raced. Animal Protection Man must have secretly slipped the **GUNGE** into his pocket before he fled. And when the thugs had given him the truth serum, he'd told them what he'd

done. And now poor Animal Protection Man had 'GONE'! So the thugs were holding Mr Parks to ransom to get the **GUNGE** from Wayne! And they'd threatened his other pets!

With his heart thumping, Wayne began to run towards his gran's house. When he got to her front gate his heart sank. Lying on the

45

garden path was Miss Purrfect's little pink collar. Fighting back the tears, Wayne dashed into the back garden. Little Warren was gone too! His playpen was empty. And pinned to his hutch was another note!

DEAR WIMP
IF YOU WANT YOUR PETS BACK TAKE THE
'YOU-KNOW-WHAT' TO THE OLD STABLES IN
ONE HOUR - BUT DON'T TRY ANYTHING SMART!
YOUR GRAN NEEDS A NEW PAIR OF SLIPPERS –
AND WE'VE GOT JUST THE THINGS TO MAKE
THEM WITH. HA! HA!

Devastated by the loss of his beloved pets and by what he'd just read, Wayne now made the decision which would change his entire life. He'd do it! He would become Johnny Catbiscuit! All right, so half an hour ago he'd been sure Animal Protection Man could find someone better than him. But there wasn't time for that now. If he was going to save his own pets and the little animals at the secret laboratory he'd just have to do it. There was no other choice. All he had to do now was get the outfit from the bin liner, put it on, say the rhyme *and* . . . he paused. Yes, that was a point! Where was the bin liner?

Wayne tried to think when he'd last seen it. He vaguely remembered Animal Protection Man trying to thrust it into his arms and him not wanting to take it. But then Animal Protection Man had dashed off . . . empty handed! So he had been left holding it! But what next? Yes! He'd dropped the bin liner on the grass as he'd clutched Mr Parks to his chest. It must still be behind the bush. Unless someone else had found it first? For instance, the thugs! For all he knew they might already have it and be lying in wait for him.

When Wayne reached the park, his lungs felt hot and raw and he had a sharp pain in his side

from running faster than he'd ever run in his whole life. He dashed over to the bush. The bin liner was gone! There was no sign of it.

'Oh no!' thought Wayne. 'Whatever am I going to do now?'

Then he felt a tap on his shoulder and a voice behind him said, 'Is this what you're looking for?'

Two seconds later, Wayne was out cold.

CHAPTER SIX
JOHNNY CATBISCUIT!

'Blooming heck, lad!' said the park keeper. 'I thought you were a goner! You gave me a real fright. Fainting like that!'

'Sorry,' said Wayne. 'You gave me a fright, too! But thanks for saving my bin liner.'

'You're welcome,' said the park keeper. 'And enjoy your fancy dress party!'

'I will!' said Wayne. 'And thanks again!'

In no time at all he was back at his gran's,

rummaging through the bin liner. First, he pulled out a magnificent sparkling silver vest with the initials 'JC' on the chest. Next came a gorgeous golden cape. After that, a pair of fabulous, winged gloves. These were followed by a pair of elegant golden boots. And finally, he pulled out an awesome silver mask and the plasma-chuffed wrist-pod.

Wayne had the wondrous super-hero outfit on in a flash. Then he took a deep breath and said:

'Be kind to your moggies and pamper your doggies
And Johnny will leave you be
But if you duff up your pups, or tease your bees
You'll answer to Johnny C!'

51

At first, nothing seemed to happen. But then he heard a low, hissing crackle and felt a sort of electric tingle rush around his body, then fizz up and down his legs a couple of times. He looked down and saw that he was actually glowing from head to toe! His entire body was surrounded by an unearthly green light which pulsed and throbbed and occasionally gave a spooky blue flicker. Then the glow disappeared. Wayne suddenly felt extraordinarily different! He dashed to his gran's big mirror to take a look at himself.

He nearly jumped out of his skin! Staring back at him, with the silver vest stretched tight

across his broad, muscular chest, was a tall, tanned, strong-jawed young man. He was staring at Wayne through piercing green eyes which positively sparkled with courage, enthusiasm, self-assurance and intelligence.

Not knowing what to say to the handsome stranger, Wayne blushed and grinned like an idiot. And, as he did, the stunningly good-looking young man copied his actions exactly.

Which was when Wayne realised that he was actually looking at himself!

'**AAAAAAAAAAGH!**' he thought. 'I'm *JOHNNY CATBISCUIT!*'

He was right. In just a few astounding

moments, he'd mutated from plain Wayne Bunn into a **REAL SUPERHERO**! How good was that? And he didn't just look different! He felt different: strong, sure of himself and alert, but totally calm, as if nothing could get him into a flap.

'Wow!' thought Johnny, admiring his handsome reflection. 'I feel great. I wish Mr Parks could see me now!'

Oh no! His poor pets! What was he doing? Preening and posing like some dimwit celeb! He must go and rescue them! **NOW**!

But there was a problem. Johnny didn't know where they were! But every second was

55

precious. He glanced anxiously at his watch. And that's when he spotted the wrist-pod and remembered Animal Protection Man's words: 'Simply use it to contact 𝕊𝕊𝕊𝕊 whenever you have a problem or a question.'

Johnny tapped in *W-0000-5H*, pressed the hash key and chose *OPTION 6*.

CHAPTER SEVEN
SUPERHERO SUPPORT SERVICE SOLUTIONS

A girl's smiling face instantly appeared on the 3D screen. She was wearing a smart green cap with an '**SSSS**' badge on it.

'Hi, Johnny!' she said. 'Thank you for calling Superhero Support Service Solutions. I'm Jatinder and I'm your Superhero Support Service Solutions Cyber-kick for today. How may I help you?'

'Well,' said Johnny. 'My pets are in terrible danger. I've got to rescue them! But I don't know where they are!'

'No probs, Johnny!' replied Jatinder. 'We can beat this one together. But first you must face some hard facts! Along with all those hundreds of other poor little stolen pets, your pals are being held in a heavily fortified secret laboratory. I'm talking CCTV, dazer-tazers, razor-lasers and multi-action harpoon launchers.'

'But I'm Johnny Catbiscuit!' said Johnny. 'I'm ready for anything. Just tell me where it is!'

'Well,' continued Jatinder, 'that's the other problem. I can't tell you where it is! Because

they constantly move it around. Its last known location was some mine-workings beneath Dead Big Mountain. But they'll have moved on again since Animal Protection Man's failed attempt to rescue the pets. Dr Septic knows

that the superheroes are always on the lookout for him and his cronies. However, we suspect that the secret laboratory may now be in the ballroom of Monstrous Manor, St Bernard Muttshoes' luxury mansion in the Wotscolds. But that could simply be a fake secret laboratory to put us off the scent. Or even a fake luxury mansion! We're dealing with very clever people here, Johnny!'

'Shivering shoelaces!' said Johnny. 'That's all I need!'

'Don't despair, Johnny!' said Jatinder. 'You will outwit them!'

'But how?' said Johnny.

'Johnny,' said Jatinder, 'your transformation from big-hearted but bashful pet-shop assistant to savvy-sophisticated-superhero is still taking place. Even as we speak, thousands of brand-new, inter-neural connections are being made on your intellectual superhighway, enhancing your knowledge and brainpower by at least a factor of five. Or, to put it more simply, you're becoming dead brainy! What's 1.5 times 3.7 divided by 6.2?'

'0.8951613,' replied Johnny, without even thinking about it.

'See what I mean!' said Jatinder. 'In addition to having superpowers and super-strength, you

are rapidly becoming a mastermind.'

'However,' continued Johnny, feeling more mind-bogglingly brainy by the moment, 'the thugs think I am still a total nitwit!'

'Exactly!' cried Jatinder. 'A doolally dingbat, desperate to get his pets back!'

'And that,' continued Wayne, 'is how I will defeat those sleazeballs!'

'Precisely!' agreed Jatinder.

Johnny glanced at his watch, then said, 'In ten minutes from now I will meet them at the Old Stables looking like a complete chump. But underneath, I will be a coiled spring, ready to unleash my super-self on those scumbuckets at

the crucial moment!'

'That's the spirit, Johnny!' cried Jatinder. 'And those scoundrels have no intention of returning your pets when you hand over the . Or even letting you out of their clutches. So you will be in terrible, terrible danger!'

'Nothing that Johnny Catbiscuit can't handle!' said Johnny, who was now feeling almost one hundred per cent Johnny Catbiscuit and hardly at all like the old Wayne Bunn.

'Johnny!' said Jatinder. 'Your goal is to get inside those secret laboratories and to finish the job that poor Animal Protection Man started! You must not fail. All animal-kind and decent folk are depending on you!'

'Just let me at them!' cried Johnny.

'Way to go, Johnny!' purred Jatinder. 'Now, is there anything else I can help you with?'

'I think that's it for now,' said Johnny. 'But I'll be in touch if I think of anything.'

'Well, thank you for calling Superhero Support Service Solutions,' said Jatinder. 'And have a super day!'

'I'll do my best!' said Johnny.

CHAPTER EIGHT
DR SEPTIC

When the **iSPLATZ-U**™ arrived at the Old Stables it was being driven by the biggest of the three thugs, but there was no sign of the others.

'Yo, dingbat!' laughed the thug, pulling up so close to Wayne that he almost crushed his toes. 'Got our messages about your soppy pets, did you? Well, have you got the **GUNGE**?'

'Yes,' said Wayne, reaching into his backpack and taking out the bottle. 'But have you got my pets?'

'Sure have!' smirked the thug, snatching the **GUNGE**. In the same instant, the smallest thug slipped out from his hiding place and grabbed Wayne by the throat.

'**AAAGH, stop it!**' gasped Wayne, doing a perfect impersonation of his old 'non-super' self. 'What are you doing? And where are my pets?'

'You bonehead!' snarled the smallest thug, as he increased his stranglehold. 'You didn't think we'd simply take the **GUNGE**, hand over your pets and let you go, did you?'

'Our bosses have plans for you, birdbrain!' said the big thug. 'Big plans! They've already got a whole laboratory full of dumb creatures,

so they thought one more wouldn't make any difference.'

And with that they bundled him into an enormous sack, tied it tight and threw him into the cage on the back of the **iSPLATZ-U**™.

After thirty minutes of bouncing along rutted cart tracks, Wayne heard the sound of large iron gates clanking open and realised that they must have arrived. Now his work would really begin.

After passing through the gates, the **iSPLATZ-U**™ bumped to a halt. An instant later, he was rolled out of the cage and taken out of the sack.

'Wake up, pet-shop boy!' snarled one of the thugs. 'This is where the fun begins!'

'Yes!' thought Wayne. 'If you only knew what sort of fun it's going to be!'

They were in the cobbled courtyard of a gigantic manor house. The entire area was guarded by a battery of lethal-looking devices,

which Wayne recognised as the dazer-tazers and razor-lasers Jatinder had warned him about. Parked a few metres away from the mansion's front doors was a huge limousine.

The front door of the manor house opened and the thugs immediately stood to attention. An incredibly tall, thin, scarecrow-like man dressed entirely in black leather emerged. He was wearing dark glasses and hanging around his neck was a doctor's stethoscope. One of his coat sleeves hung limply by his side. Sticking out of it was a false hand. In his other, real hand, he carried a huge and fearsome-looking scalpel dripping fresh blood.

It was Dr Septic! The ruthless maniac whose acts of violence, cruelty and wickedness had struck terror into the hearts of animals and decent folk for decades. And into Wayne's own heart, ever since he was knee high to a spaniel.

Dr Septic was followed by a very short and fat man wearing a massive ankle-length rabbit-skin coat, fur boots and one of those gruesome fur hats which still has the animal's head and tail attached to it.

'And that,' thought Wayne, 'must be the detestable St Bernard Muttshoes!'

The two sleazebags came over to Wayne and the thugs. Dr Septic looked at Wayne as if he

were something you might find in a blocked drain, then poked him with the toe of his boot. In a harsh, cracked voice, which made Wayne think of someone scrubbing their teeth with a broken brick, he looked at the biggest thug and said, 'Did you get it?'

'Sure did, boss!' replied the thug and handed him the **GUNGE**.

As Dr Septic reached for it, the joint of his false hand gave a sharp squeak, reminding Wayne of the game he'd so innocently played just hours earlier.

'OK! Bring him in!' growled Dr Septic. 'We'll get to work right away!'

The thugs pushed Wayne through the front door of the mansion then, along a gloomy corridor. With Dr Septic and St Bernard leading the way, they eventually arrived at a pair of huge double doors with the word **BALLROOM** on them.

However, when they opened the doors, it was plain to see that this was no ballroom. It was more like a torture chamber! The walls of Dr Septic's massive laboratory were lined with hundreds of cages containing all manner of stolen pets, including rabbits, hamsters, kittens, white mice, chickens, puppies and gerbils. Most of them were cowering in their cells, whimpering pathetically. At the end of the room was a huge

73

filing cabinet marked **WORK IN PROGRESS**. It had dozens of drawers, each one labelled with horrendous-sounding names like: **TEN-LEGGED PIGLETS, HYPER-SLOTHS, BONSAI DONKEYS, HAIRY GOLDFISH, PIT-BULL BEDBUGS, GLOW-IN-THE DARK FERRETS, REVERSIBLE LIZARDS** and **PRE-FLATTENED HEDGEHOGS**. Animal Protection Man hadn't

74

been exaggerating!

Wayne suddenly heard excited barking and, at the far corner of the laboratory, he saw his beloved Mr Parks! He was locked in a tiny cage. And, next to that, was a hutch containing Miss Purrfect and Warren! Wayne's eyes grew moist and his heart went out to his little chums.

As Wayne gazed longingly at his dear pets,

75

Dr Septic took out his horrible scalpel and growled, 'Just thought we'd let you see your pals one last time. OK, boys! Take him to the operating theatre! We'll be along in a moment.'

'What are you going to do to me?' groaned Wayne as the thugs bundled him towards the door.

'Well, pet-shop boy,' murmured St Bernard Muttshoes in a horrid, slobbery voice, which made Wayne think of a hippopotamus wallowing in warm hair gel. 'We want to do a little experiment with the **GUNGE**. And you're the perfect candidate! What's more, now that Animal Protection Man is taken care of, we

won't have to worry about any interfering superheroes spoiling our fun, will we? We'll just take our time and do entirely as we please!'

'And if it all goes wrong,' laughed Dr Septic, 'it won't matter. After all, no one's going to miss a waste of space like you, are they?'

CHAPTER NINE
TIME FOR ACTION!

The thugs marched Wayne down the corridor to a door marked OPERATING THEATRE, then pushed him inside.

'Right, dingbat!' said the bigger one, taking out a nasty-looking syringe. 'Let's get you ready for Dr Septic. Roll up your sleeve!'

Wayne knew it was time for action. 'Anything you say,' he replied in his most pathetic 'Wayne Bunn' voice.

Then, in one lightning-fast movement, he ripped off his tracksuit and trainers, instantly revealing his magnificent Johnny Catbiscuit outfit and yelling,

'Surprise, surprise! I was in disguise. Now, both of you . . . try this for size!'

And, as his astonished captors watched his stunning transformation from simpleton to superhero

79

in open-mouthed amazement, Johnny elbowed the biggest one in the face and stamped on the other's foot. While they howled with pain and rage, he dashed out of the operating theatre and down the corridor. Then, making sure he didn't get too far ahead of the thugs, who had now begun to race after him, he sprinted into the courtyard.

The thugs followed him into the daylight, but then came to a halt and peered around, baffled. There was no sign of Johnny anywhere. It was as if he'd vanished into thin air. They scratched their heads in bewilderment. And that's when Johnny dropped down from the ledge above the

doors, slipped back inside and slammed them firmly shut.

As the furious thugs began hurling themselves at the doors, yelling all sorts of bloodcurdling curses and threats, Johnny sprinted over to the control panel he'd spotted earlier and located the switches for the powerful razor-lasers and dazer-tazers which guarded the courtyard. He now had the thugs entirely at his mercy. If he'd wanted to, he could have wiped them out at the flick of a switch. But there was already too much pain and suffering in the world. And it wasn't Johnny Catbiscuit's job to add to it. Only to protect the innocent and bring the

guilty to justice.

So, instead of pressing the button marked razor-lasers, he flicked the one which operated the dazer-tazers. As bolts of blue lightning crackled from the barrels of the dazer-tazers and an ear-splitting screech filled the air, the thugs began to whirl in confusion, clutching their heads and gibbering like idiots. Two seconds later they were both lying on the cobbles, out of action.

'OK, that's them sorted!' thought Johnny, flicking the switch off. 'Now I'll go look for their masters!'

But there was no need! He heard the sound

of running footsteps and saw Dr Septic appear at the opposite end of the long corridor. He was carrying a lethal-looking, multi-barrelled harpoon launcher! There was a series of bangs, followed by several blinding flashes and a whole load of glittering steel-spikes were suddenly speeding towards Johnny.

A split second before the savage stakes skewered him, Johnny performed a two-footed, two-metre-high leap into the air that would have made a jump jet jealous! Then, with his elbows and knees firmly wedged against the corridor walls, he watched the missiles pass harmlessly beneath him. He dropped back to

83

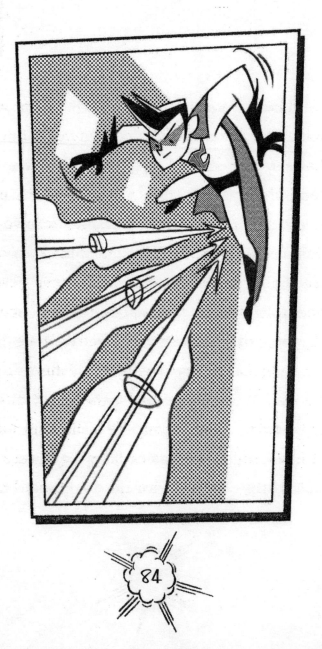

84

the floor, intending to rush at Dr Septic and overpower him before he could reload. But at that moment he heard a shout and saw St Bernard Muttshoes appear at the opposite end of the corridor with four large, ferocious-looking men in white coats. All of the men had exactly the same enormous box-shaped heads, blonde crewcuts and square-rimmed specs. They were armed with long electric prods.

Seeing he was outnumbered, Johnny took the only route left to him and dashed into a large sitting room, where the walls were hung with enormous tapestries showing scenes of bull-fighting and bear-baiting. St Bernard and

his henchmen followed him. The four bizarre boffins soon had Johnny backed up against a tapestry, thrusting their glowing prods at him and grinning at the thought of grilling him alive.

But Johnny **EXPLODED** into action, flattening two of them with his windmilling right fist and flooring the others by **BANGING** their heads together. As they collapsed in a heap, their prods came into contact, instantly **SHORT-CIRCUITING** and **ELECTRO-FRAZZLING** the four freaks in a spectacular shower of sparks!

At that moment, there was the sound of footsteps. Dr Septic must have reloaded his

harpoon gun and be on the warpath again!

'He's here, in the lounge!' screamed St Bernard. But then he saw the blazing tapestries, which had been set alight by the sparks from the electric prods, and yelled, 'Fire! Fire!'

And that's exactly what Dr Septic did as he entered the room. He fired one of the terrible harpoons into his abominable partner's stomach.

As the doomed St Bernard slumped to the floor and gasped his last gasp, Dr Septic retreated. He was out of ammunition and choking on the smoke from the blaze.

In other circumstances Johnny would have let Monstrous Manor burn to the ground, but he had yet to rescue the little animals. He hurled himself at the flames, using his fire-resistant super-suit to smother them before they could take hold. Then, when he was certain they were out, he went to find the evil genius.

But there was no sign of Dr Septic. Realising he'd finally met his match, he had fled. The hunter was now the hunted!

Dr Septic had the advantage. The house was huge and he knew his way round its dozens of rooms and maze of corridors. He could be hiding anywhere. Johnny decided there was nothing for it but to search the place, room by room.

But then he got his lucky break. He'd just searched the empty library when he heard a familiar sound.

CHAPTER TEN
SQUEAK! SQUEAK!

The sound seemed to be coming from behind a bookshelf-covered wall. Johnny went over and listened. There it was again. **SQUEAK! SQUEAK!** He reached out to move a couple of books so he could investigate further. But his hand simply slid across a flat, smooth surface.

There weren't any bookshelves! Just very realistic paintings of books and bookshelves! It was a false wall. If Johnny could have been

bothered looking for it, he would have probably found the secret switch which opened it. But he hadn't time for that. So he simply gave the 'bookshelves' an almighty two-fisted **PUNCH**, powerful enough to make the whole house rattle. And the entire wall collapsed in a whirl of plaster and dust.

Standing on the other side, clutching the bottle of **GUNGE**, was Dr Septic.

'Ah, there you are, Dr Septic!' said Johnny. 'I didn't know you played hide and squeak, too!'

Dr Septic looked puzzled for a moment, then said, 'Well, you've found me. And I suppose you want this back!'

91

And he threw the **GUNGE** across the
library. Johnny took his eyes off him for all of
two seconds. But that was all Dr Septic needed!
Scrambling over what was left of the wall, he

hurled himself through the windows, landing in the courtyard in a shower of broken glass.

Johnny was after him in a **FLASH**. And this time he wasn't taking any chances! Deliberately positioning himself between Dr Septic and his limousine, he now began to close in on him.

'So, who are you anyway?' asked Dr Septic, as he calmly rose to his feet and began to brush off his clothes.

'Catbiscuit's the name,' said Johnny. 'Johnny Catbiscuit! You know, Dr Septic, when I was very little, my gran used to say to me, "If you're bad, Dr Septic will get you!" But I never was

bad. You're the one who's always been bad. And now I've got you!'

'I think not,' snarled Dr Septic, suddenly looking extremely confident and staring past Johnny's shoulder. 'You have miscalculated, Mr Catbiscuit. I have one more associate who you haven't accounted for. He is now standing just a few metres behind you. And he has a gun pointed at the back of your head. At the first signal from me, he will release the safety catch. Then, at the second, he will pull the trigger.'

'You're bluffing!' said Johnny, not daring to take his eyes off Dr Septic for even one second. 'All of your accomplices are taken care of.'

'Am I?' smiled Dr Septic. Then he looked over Johnny's shoulder once more, nodded and said, 'OK, Manfred, release the safety catch!'

From somewhere just behind him, Johnny heard a loud click and he froze.

Before Dr Septic could give his second signal, Johnny whirled around, hit the ground and rolled across the courtyard.

But no shot came.

Because there was no one there. Just Dr Septic's huge limousine. And when Johnny picked himself up, Dr Septic had vanished!

'Suffering sea lions!' gasped Johnny. 'I've lost him!'

Dr Septic had fooled him. He'd simply put his hand into his pocket and clicked the remote locking tab on his car key. The click of the 'safety catch' had actually been the latches snapping open on his limousine.

'Yes, Dr Septic,' thought Johnny with a smile. 'You may have got away today. But there'll be many more occasions when our paths cross. And *I've* still got a lot to learn.'

CHAPTER ELEVEN
TONGUES

When Johnny went back into the mansion and reached the door of the secret laboratory, he was suddenly aware of a terrible silence on the other side. He couldn't hear a chirrup, a miaow or a woof. Not a sound! 'Oh no,' he thought. 'I'm too late! Dr Septic must have done something terrible to all the poor little animals before he fled.' And that would mean Johnny's own pets would be . . . No, the idea was too

terrible to think about! Heart racing, he pushed open the door, dreading what he'd find on the other side.

But, the moment he walked inside, he was met with a deafening round of hooting, whistling, barking and flapping. All of the little animals were joyously leaping around their cages, turning somersaults, clapping their paws, wagging their tails and squeaking with delight. And every single one of them was looking at *him*!

Johnny raced round the laboratory, snapping locks off the cages, lifting out the overjoyed little captives, patting them reassuringly, then gently

setting them down on the floor. Finally he came to his own pets. They recognised him instantly, as he knew they would, even though he was still one hundred per cent Johnny

Catbiscuit! The moment they were free, they went berserk, jumping about, licking his face and rolling over on their backs for their tums to be tickled.

Johnny was over the moon! He'd succeeded! He'd completed the job which Animal Protection Man had begun! Well, almost! All that remained now was for him to return the animals to their homes. But then he thought of something. Something which could well take the shine off his day of triumph.

He hadn't the faintest idea where any of them lived! However was he going to return them to their heartbroken owners? There were

hundreds of them! It could take him forever! What a problem!

Problem? What was he thinking of? Johnny hit the keys on his wrist-pod and Jatinder's smiling face instantly appeared on the screen.

'Hello, Johnny!' she said. 'From where I'm sitting it looks like you have been successful on your first mission. So, please accept sincerest congratulations from all of us here at Superhero Support Service Solutions. It's cream cakes all round today, thanks to you!'

From somewhere in the background Johnny heard muffled cheering and wild shouts of '**LONG LIVE JOHNNY CATBISCUIT! LONG LIVE**

JOHNNY CATBISCUIT!'

As the noise died down, Jatinder continued, 'The only superhero ever to have achieved such great things on their first ever mission was the legendary Cardigan Bootstop. So now you have a lot to live up to! But we have great hopes for you, Johnny. Great hopes! Now, how may I help you?'

'Well, Jatinder,' said Johnny. 'I've freed all these little creatures. But I don't know where they live.'

'Not a problem!' said Jatinder. 'Simply ask them.'

'But how?' said Johnny.

'For you, Johnny, it will be a piece of cake!'

said Jatinder. 'As part of your superhero upgrade programme you are about to receive the gift of tongues. Many, many tongues!'

Johnny gulped, then said, 'But how will they all fit in my mouth, Jatinder? I've hardly got room for the one I've got now!'

'No, not real tongues!' cried Jatinder. 'It is just a way of saying you will be able to speak with all manner of creatures in their own languages.'

'Wow, how cool is that!' exclaimed Johnny.

'Yes, I know!' went on Jatinder. 'Isn't it? To begin with you will know just enough to get by. But in time you will improve. Before his sad decline, Animal Protection Man had become

fluent in almost all animal languages, including wildebeest, stinkbug, koala and Great Danish. The only ones he never mastered were tadpole and aardvark. But they have different alphabets from us.'

'Yes, he told me he talked to the animals!' said Johnny. 'Now, I'll get busy returning these little pets to their humans. They'll be back home in a flash.'

'Sure thing!' said Jatinder. 'But, Johnny, a word of warning! Remember . . . Dr Septic is still at large. He has friends everywhere! So, once you have completed your mission, you must resume your old life as plain Wayne

Bunn. From now on, you will live a double life,
spending your days as Wayne, but becoming
superhero Johnny Catbiscuit whenever you are
needed. And with Dr Septic and his hench-people
on the loose that will be often, I assure you!
Now, is there anything else I can help you with?'

'I think that's it for now,' said Johnny. 'But I'll be in touch if anything comes up.'

'Yes, do that, Johnny,' purred Jatinder. 'And thank you for calling Superhero Support Service Solutions. Have a super afternoon, Johnny!'

'I'll do my best!' said Johnny.

CHAPTER TWELVE
FELIX PAWSON

As Jatinder faded from the screen, Johnny looked at all the creatures gathered around him. Then he spoke to them, very, very slowly. 'Listen everyone!' he said. 'I am going to reunite you with your loved ones. But, before I can do that you must tell me where you live. Do . . . you . . . understand . . . me?'

All of the little animals nodded – apart from the one-eyed tortoise, which just remained

very quiet and thoughtful.

A very cute, wire-haired terrier now trotted up to Johnny, looked up at him and yapped, 'My name's Rex. First of all, on behalf of myself and all the other animals, I'd like to thank you for rescuing us with such dog-ged courage and determination! From what would have been a cat-astrophe! Ha ha ha! Do you get it? And by the way, I live at the sweetshop on the High Street. With old Mrs Pipsqueak.'

'Wow!' gasped Johnny. 'I just understood every single word you said!'

'And I understood every single word you just said!' replied Rex. 'Yes, it's good to talk, isn't it,

Johnny Catbiscuit?'

And then, one after another, all the other animals told Johnny where they lived.

Followed by dozens of joyously yapping, purring, squeaking, chirruping animals, Johnny flung open the ballroom doors and bounded along the corridor. He was utterly elated by his success and totally intent on completing his mission, the first of what he hoped would be many glorious missions to come.

Such was the young superhero's eagerness and joy that he now made the two mistakes which almost cost him his life. So keen was he to finish his great adventure that he a) didn't

take the trouble to check that the coast was clear and b) rather stupidly assumed that every single one of his enemies had either fled the scene or had been put out of action. And, as he would say over and over again in years to come, 'Never, ever assume *anything*!' Or, as he preferred to put it,

'*The superhero who fails to check*
Is bound to get it in the neck!
So always be completely sure
Your foes aren't coming back for more!'

But this time he didn't. Which is why, to the little animals' horror, one of the thugs Johnny had so *kindly* spared from the razor-lasers

earlier now hit him with the force of an express train. Such force that, for a fraction of a second, Johnny was caught off-balance. Which was just long enough for another thug to seize his arms and pin them to his sides.

Then the first thug drew back the plunger on a giant hypodermic syringe marked '**LETHAL**' and prepared to fill his veins with a shot of extremely toxic serum. A shot which would have brought Johnny's long and illustrious superhero career to a tragic end before it had even begun! Had it not been for the cat.

For, as all of the other creatures recoiled in shock and terror, whimpering and mewling

with fear, a *HISSING, SPITTING FIREBALL* of **FUR 'N' FURY** landed on the shoulders of the biggest thug. This positive **tYPhOON** of **TEETH** and **claws** then proceeded to bite and scratch his

large and fleshy neck so viciously and mercilessly
that he let out an almighty **YELL** and rammed
the giant needle home. Not into Johnny's arm,

114

but into the other thug's arm. Which caused *him* to slump to the floor with a groan, releasing his hold on Johnny.

Then *Johnny* **WALLOPED** the big thug with such a **humdinger** of a **punch** that it actually lifted him a metre into the air and he flew to the opposite side of the room. All of which brought a round of applause from the animals.

This time, Johnny *triple*-checked that the thugs were most *definitely* and *permanently* out of action and turned to his rescuer, a strikingly handsome, bluish-grey tom cat. A strikingly handsome, bluish-grey tom cat which was now coolly washing its face and paws, as if it had

115

just done nothing more than polish off a rather tasty dish of catfood.

'Thanks,' said Johnny. 'I would have been a goner without your help. As I was saying only twenty minutes ago, I've still got a lot to learn.'

'No probs,' purred the cat, without even bothering to look up. 'It's cool.'

Then, having finished its wash, it did look up at Johnny, calmly adding, 'I've never liked those pesky needles. Not since some human took me to the vets for my cat-flu jab when I was an itty-bitty little kitty. And I also had a score to settle with those two thugs. Ever since they kitnapped me and my twin brother so long

ago that I've forgotten who we actually belonged to in the first place!'

'So,' said Johnny, an idea beginning to form in his mind as he looked at this remarkable, *super*-cool and *super*-intelligent animal. 'Does that mean that you're homeless?'

'I suppose it does,' said the cat. 'Why, have you got something in mind?'

'I certainly have!' said Johnny. 'But what about your twin brother?'

'Oh, Roland,' said the cat, suddenly taking a close interest in one of its paws. 'He sort of "went over to the opposition", if you take my meaning?'

'What, Dr Septic's lot?' said Johnny.

'Got it in one!' said the cat. 'Our Roland's now living in the lap of luxury. Or, to be precise, the lap of the evil genius himself.' He shrugged. 'But hey, whatever! I suppose it's just different strokes for different furry folks!'

Then the cat held out its paw, and said, 'Pawson's the name, Felix Pawson. Glad to have been of help.'

And so began a very long, very happy and very successful partnership between Johnny Catbiscuit and the extremely cool and infinitely courageous cat called Felix Pawson. The extremely cool and infinitely courageous cat

who, after receiving some superpowers of his own, would soon be sharing all sorts of astonishing adventures with him. They would vanquish villains, zap sleazeballs and bring comfort, salvation and hope to hundreds of animals and humans around the world.

So, starting as they meant to go on, Johnny and Felix set about returning the stolen pets to their humans or, in the case of the wild animals, the woods and fields. And all at positively supersonic speeds! Because, by now, Johnny was really beginning to find his superhero feet! Or, to be more accurate, his superhero *wings*!

CHAPTER THIRTEEN
WHOOOOOOOOOOOSH!

Yes! Just as Animal Protection Man had promised (and in one fell 'swoop', as Johnny later liked to think of it) he discovered that he was able to fly! Not by rushing about and leaping into the air. Or even by wildly flapping his arms, as Animal Protection Man had done. But simply by deciding he was going to fly. Just as you or I would decide we're going to walk, or run, or sit! So, one minute he was earthbound. And the

next, he was airborne! And rather than being a complicated matter, involving all sorts of fiddly manoeuvres, hard-to-master techniques and arduous training, the entire thing was a piece of cake! Johnny simply thought 'I want to go higher'. And he went higher! Or 'I want to go faster'. And he went faster! He was a born (again) natural!

And to say the whole experience was an 'absolute blast!' would be like describing the discovery that you could walk through walls, read other people's thoughts, or become invisible as, 'quite interesting'. For Johnny, being able to fly was completely

121

STUPENDOUS!

AWESOME!

MIND-BOGGLING!

WONDERFUL!

And utterly, utterly
LIBERATING!

If he'd had the time, he might well have gone
for an experimental thousand-kilometre spin,
perhaps taking in the beautiful Wotscolds

and the sights of
Londonland on the
way! But Johnny
was a superhero. And
superheroes do not

122

neglect their responsibilities and duties! So, rather than trying out loop-the-loops, nap-of-the-earth* trips and barrel rolls, he got busy reuniting the pets with their homes and owners.

With the little critters cosily stowed in his extremely roomy 'Wayne Bunn' backpack, he made trip after trip after trip. And all at lickety-split speeds. Of course, for the bigger animals, like the donkey, the

* the technique by which Johnny would fly just a few metres above the ground, hugging the contours of the earth — a strategy he would come to use in many of his adventures.

Great Dane dog and the pair of Flemish Giant rabbits, it was a different matter, involving more personalised, but nevertheless extremely speedy, trips!

In fact, aided by Felix Pawson's phenomenal animal-management skills, Johnny had the whole job done in the blink of an eye!

And what a joy it was to see the looks on the faces of the astounded owners as the handsome young superhero handed them the little creatures which they'd truly believed they'd never see again. There were shrieks of joy, squeaks of joy and tears and hugs all round. And, when it was over, Johnny and Felix knew it was a job well done. Pets reunited!

Then, remembering Jatinder's warning, Johnny reverted to his old Wayne Bunn self and set off for his gran's, pausing only to pop into a phone box and make a quick call.

'Now, chaps!' he said, in his newly-acquired tongues, as he let his own pets (old and new)

into the house. 'I've one more errand to run. Then I think you lot are due for some quality-time treats!'

'Hide and squeak!' barked Mr Parks.

'Chasing string!' purred Miss Purrfect.

'Lettuce!' whispered Warren.

'A supersonic flight around the Realms of Normality!' said Felix Pawson.

'It's a promise!' said Wayne. Then he set off for the hospital.

When he arrived at the reception area, he saw a group of people clustered around the TV, chattering excitedly. Glancing up at the screen, he saw a reporter holding a microphone out to

an old lady with a wire-haired terrier sitting on her lap. It was Mrs Pipsqueak and Rex!

'And could you describe the person who returned your Rex?' said the reporter.

'He was wearing a silver mask,' said Mrs Pipsqueak. 'But you could tell he was really handsome underneath it. Ooh, what a hero! He saved my Rex!'

'Yes, viewers!' said the reporter. 'The mysterious stranger also saved hundreds more pets like Rex! But who is the handsome masked hero? We know he has the initials JC on his silver vest. And we also know, thanks to an anonymous telephone call, that St Bernard

Muttshoes was a total rotter. A rotter who, along with all those scumballs up at Monstrous Manor, has finally got what he deserves. But we still don't know the whereabouts of the evil Dr Septic. Or the whereabouts of the precious life-saving **GUNGE**!'

As the onlookers '**OOHED**!' and '**AAHED**!' at the unfolding news of Johnny's heroic exploits, Wayne set off down the corridor to the intensive-care ward where his gran was. Halfway along it, he met the tall, distinguished-looking doctor who was trying to find a cure for his gran's poorly heart.

'Ah, young Wayne Bunn!' she exclaimed.

'Come to see your gran, have you?'

'Yes, I have, Doctor,' said Wayne. 'I know she's unconscious but I thought I'd sit with her for a while.'

'I'm sure she'll appreciate that,' said the doctor.

'Oh, by the way, Doctor,' said Wayne, as he handed her the bottle of **GUNGE**, 'I found this on my way in. I think someone probably dropped it.'

And that was more or less it.

Wayne Bunn became Johnny Catbiscuit. Felix Pawson became his loyal sidekick (and acquired some rather remarkable super-skills along the way!).

The pets were rescued. Hundreds of people, including Wayne's gran, were saved by the GUNGE. And the baddies – with the exception of the evil Dr Septic – got what was coming to them.

But there was still one little mystery which Wayne was puzzling over as he sat in front of the TV later that evening, watching the news of Johnny's daring deeds.

As he'd left the hospital, he'd spotted a small

and very battered-looking, bearded old man being helped from an ambulance into a wheel-chair. The man was covered in cuts and bruises, his clothes were torn and filthy, and he looked completely exhausted. But there was something familiar about him. As they passed each other, the man looked up at Wayne and winked, then put up his thumb and mouthed the words, 'Well done, lad! I knew you could do it!'

THE END

SUPERHERO PROFILE

Animal Protection Man

Animal Protection Man (59) first became aware of his 'calling' when, at the age of five, he brought his pet stickleback 'back from the dead'. He gave him the kiss of life after he'd leapt out of his tank, flipped and flopped across the living-room carpet and tried to climb inside the TV set, having mistaken it

for an aquarium (an understandable error, especially as *Finding Nemo* was on at the time). NB It was the stickleback who leapt out of his tank, not Animal Protection Man.

DAY-TO-DAY IDENTITY

Bald, bearded, bespectacled animal psychologist Philip Cansdale. He treats deranged ducks, batty bats, claustrophobic moles, eagles with vertigo, trout who're terrified of water, tadpoles who think they're punctuation marks and more barmy beasts.

PETS

An Old English Sheepdog called Philip, an Abyssinian guinea pig (also called Philip), a

furry caterpillar (Philip) and a Tibetan yak (known as Philip).

SPECIAL POWERS

Can speak over 400 animal languages, including anteater, alligator and aphid. Phenomenal strength and super-keen eyesight – for example, he can spot a distressed daddy-long-legs from four miles away. He is also a leading light in the rapidly-growing art of 'cat-whispering'.

An extremely swift and agile flyer, able to copy the flight styles of most airborne creatures, including swallows, hover-flies, bumblebees, condors and pipistrelle bats.

Once acted as 'lead bird' to a flock of geese, ducks, blue tits and tree pipits, who were being pursued by a gang of gourmet chefs in micro-light aircraft, finally guiding them to safety.

Also able to see in the dark through a combination of hyper-acute eyesight and the little sonic 'beeps' he emits, which tend to make him sound like a reversing lorry, whenever he's echo-locating.

FIRST EVER SUPER-MISSION

To the annual Moose-Hurling event in the Snowberian settlement of Old Bones Creek, in which the village strong-men compete to see who can throw a moose the furthest.

135

Wrapped in cotton-wool, the moose are hurled on to enormous comfy mattresses and afterwards fed carrots and bran mash, then tickled affectionately. Nevertheless, Animal Protection Man was determined to stamp out this barbaric practice which, whilst not actually harming the moose physically, does tremendous damage to their personal dignity and self-esteem. So, disguised as a giant spruce tree, Animal Protection Man hid himself in the forest, then, as the hurling started, dashed out from his hiding place and caught each plummeting moose. Then he handed them over to his sidekick, Vegetarian Girl, who led

the startled beasts to safety, followed by a short course in assertiveness training and a slap-up banquet of willow-buds drenched in maple-leaf syrup. Animal Protection Man then gave the hurlers a good talking-to! This seems to have worked as they now only hurl environmentally friendly 'inflatable' moose.

CURRENT STATUS

Now retired, but does voluntary work at the St Rolfus of Ozissi Extremely Poorly Pet Hospital.

NB: The plural of moose is moose, not meese, as some people seem to think. However, the plural of goose . . .

VILLAIN PROFILE

Dr Septacemius J. Septic

PHYSICAL APPEARANCE

Dr Septic is extremely tall, thin and evil, and is fond of wearing clothes and jewellery made from the skins and other bits and pieces of endangered species.

FAMILY BACKGROUND

No one's sure who Dr Septic's parents were,

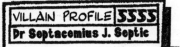

but lurking somewhere in the tangled branches of his family tree are several Medieval Hag-Burners, Erik the Human Meat Cleaver (the Scourge of Snowberia), an entire clan of head-hunting cannibals and a werewolf called Boris. However, others believe him to be a laboratory experiment gone wrong.

NOTABLE PHYSICAL CHARACTERISTICS

At the age of fifteen, Dr Septic lost his left hand whilst attempting to steal the contents of a St Rolfus of Ozissi Poorly Pet charity box. When his thieving fingers became jammed in the box's very narrow slot, determined not to be caught 'red-handed', the young Trevor

Septic slowly gnawed through his own wrist. He escaped, leaving his trapped fist in the slot. This caused a passing member of the public to become clinically unzipped when they spotted this gruesome sight, especially as the sign on the box said, 'PLEASE GIVE GENEROUSLY OR, AT LEAST, LEND A HAND!' Since then, Dr Septic has had more than twenty false hands, naming each one and keeping it in a glove by his bed.

FIRST EVIL DEED

Dr Septic first realised his evil calling when, at the age of six, he discovered that stealing the cuddly toys from smaller children, then

slowly ripping them to pieces gave him a great deal of personal satisfaction. Aged seven he began his lifelong habit of helping old ladies across the road then, halfway across, stealing their walking frames and spectacles and running off, leaving them stranded in the middle of several lanes of roaring traffic.

HENCHPEOPLE

Dr Septic has a huge retinue of hangers-on, admirers, fellow conspirators and outright creeps, including Professor Elvis Troll, Spitting Cuthbert, Murgatroyd Doom, Fenella Fiendish, Mr Nicely-Nicely, Vladimir Truss and Janice Evil, his girlfriend and the mother

of his gormless stepson, Gluey Hughie. All of them carry his signed photo, which they kiss each night, before drifting off to sleep.

SECRET HIDEAWAY

Dr Septic's hideaway, is a huge moated fortress, Septic Towers, where he lives on Rose Poochong tea, paracetamol, earwig-butter crunch and song-thrush paté. When he isn't dreaming up wicked schemes to destroy the superheroes, conquer the Realms of Normality and enslave its good and decent inhabitants, Dr Septic spends his time stroking his cat Roland and throwing baby hamsters and ducklings to the enormous

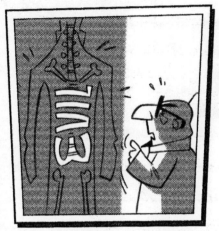

crocogators which live in his moat.

FINAL EVIL FACT

Universally acknowledged to be the most evil being on Space-Speck Earth, Dr Septic says he has the word 'EVIL' written all the way through him, just like a stick of rock. His doctor Professor Elvis Troll doubted this until he X-rayed him and found it was true!

KERPOW!
THE ULTIMATE SUPERHERO'S HANDBOOK

UNCOVER YOUR INNER SUPERHERO!

EVERYTHING YOU'VE EVER WANTED TO KNOW ABOUT BECOMING A SUPERHERO

(but were too much of a wimp to ask)

STAGE ONE - SELF DISCOVERY
HAVE YOU GOT WHAT IT TAKES TO BECOME SUPERHUMAN?

Some people are perfect superhero material, almost as if they're born to become super-heroes! However, these sorts of people are very, very rare. Others have the potential to be 'special', but need a huge dollop of tremendous

144

good fortune to cross that line which separates the simply 'gifted and talented' from the **stupendously, mind-boggling, awesomely, earth-shatteringly SUPER!** And others, sadly, don't stand a pilchard in a piranha pond's chance of becoming a superhero.

So, to find out if you've got what it takes to become a caped crusader or dynamic daredevil, simply take the following test.

Disclaimer: I .... [print your name here] do realise that by taking this test I may discover things which could change my life forever, possibly even setting me on the glittering path to becoming a top superhero. If this does happen, I agree to pay Michael Cox and Egmont Press five million pounds. Signed ....

THE TEST

1 HAVE YOU GOT ANY OF THE FOLLOWING EXTRAS, OR SPECIAL BODY BITS?

A) a third leg or more than two eyes

B) a huge furry tail which enables you to dangle upside down from satellite dishes and frighten people in tall buildings

C) nice hair

D) dry skin

2 HAVE YOU EVER GONE:

A) invisible

B) radioactive and hexagon-shaped

C) a bit sleepy

D) to the shops for your mum

3 HAVE YOU EVER SEEN YOUR PARENTS OR GRANDPARENTS WEARING:

A) spangled lurex jumpsuits or psychoplasmic translucent body armour

B) invisibility belts

C) thermal underwear

D) beige cardigans

4 IF PEOPLE ARE IN TROUBLE, DO THEY:

A) beg you to help them

B) call you only when there's no one else to turn to

C) avoid you because they know if you get involved, things will only get a thousand times worse

D) blame you for the mess they're in

5 | HAVE YOU HAD ANY OF THE FOLLOWING EXPERIENCES:

➡️ **A)** you can't reach the soap in the bath so you simply make it leap from the soap dish into your hands by concentrating really hard

➡️ **B)** in a race on school sports day you reach the finishing line before the other competitors have even taken their first step

➡️ **C)** people fall asleep while you are telling them about a really exciting adventure you've just had

➡️ **D)** if you accidentally step on a crack between the paving stones when walking down the street, you have to make yourself go back and start again

148

6 ARE YOU ABLE TO:

A) run up sheer walls with the ease of a house fly

B) run in slow motion

C) run up sheer walls with the knees of a house fly

D) run up a huge phone bill

7 IF YOU HAD A SIDEKICK WOULD YOU PREFER THEM TO BE:

A) a boy

B) a girl

C) an animal

D) your mum

DISCOVER YOUR PERSONAL SUPER POTENTIAL STATUS

MOSTLY As: You are most probably an absolutely perfect candidate for becoming a superhero. However, checks would have to be carried out on your family background and ancestors. And if any of your relatives were a) a zombie b) a tram driver c) a vampire c) a member of the Britsh royal family or d) a werewolf, you would be instantly disqualified. However, to save yourself the expense of having your ancestors investigated, there are

150

a few checks you can carry out yourself.

For instance, if you use the word 'absolutely' more than twice a week, secretly enjoy snacking on pet food, or are excited by the word 'pamphlet', you can forget any ideas you may have entertained about becoming 'super'.

MOSTLY **Bs:** You've got something about you that sets you aside from run-of-the-mill ordinary people. You may already be aware of this. Perhaps people point you out to their friends who then ask you for your autograph. Or maybe your teachers address you as 'your fabulousness'? However, in no way does this

mean that you're cut out to be a superhero. All right, you may well become one of those people who are really good at waving, having their photograph taken, and pouting in an 'interesting' manner. But that's probably as far as it goes. The world of superheroes is full of exceptional people. And you don't even touch first base!

MOSTLY Cs: Goodness! You are an ordinary bundle of proteins, chemicals and electric impulses, aren't you? How do you get through the day without boring yourself comatose? You no doubt like counting things, for instance the hairs on the head of the person in front of you

when you're queuing at The Most Boring Shop in the World. And you probably love tidying up your collection of 'fascinating' old coffee cups. Why don't you become a sleep therapist or a snooker player?

MOSTLY Ds: Oh dear! To be brutally honest, you have superhero negative-equity. Even with intensive training, a complete body transplant and daily infusions of kinetic hyper-energy you would still be the sort of superhero who leaves people in a far worse predicament than you found them. Sorry, but it looks like you'd be much better off as a local government officer.

EGMONT PRESS: ETHICAL PUBLISHING

Egmont Press is about turning writers into successful authors and children into passionate readers – producing books that enrich and entertain. As a responsible children's publisher, we go even further, considering the world in which our consumers are growing up.

Safety First
Naturally, all of our books meet legal safety requirements. But we go further than this; every book with play value is tested to the highest standards – if it fails, it's back to the drawing-board.

Made Fairly
We are working to ensure that the workers involved in our supply chain – the people that make our books – are treated with fairness and respect.

Responsible Forestry
We are committed to ensuring all our papers come from environmentally and socially responsible forest sources.

For more information, please visit our website at
www.egmont.co.uk/ethicalpublishing

The Forest Stewardship Council (FSC) is an international, non-governmental organisation dedicated to promoting responsible management of the world's forests. FSC operates a system of forest certification and product labelling that allows consumers to identify wood and wood-based products from well-managed forests.

For more information about the FSC, please visit their website at www.fsc-uk.org